# A Cat and a Dog Go into Space

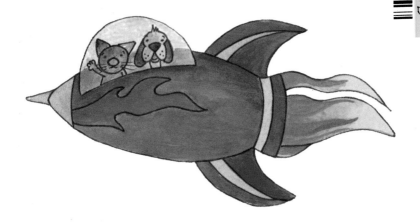

Story by Kris Bonnell

Pictures by Michelle Kemper Brownlow

We are going into space.

2

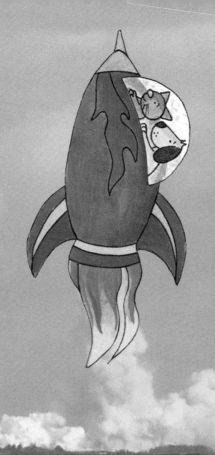

We are going by the clouds.

4

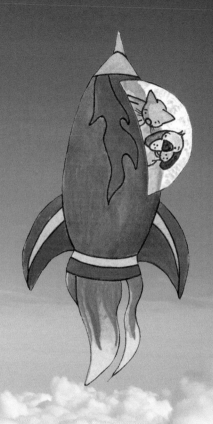

We see the stars.

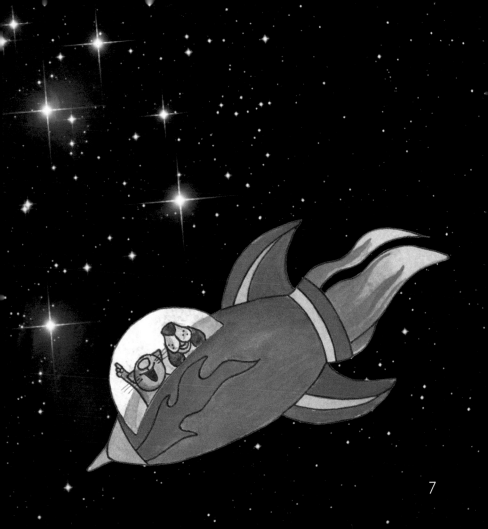

We see the moon.

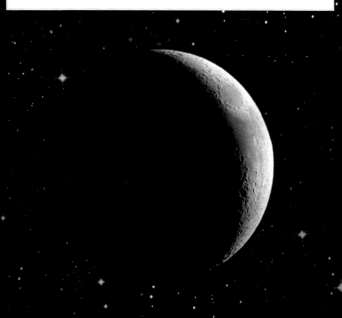

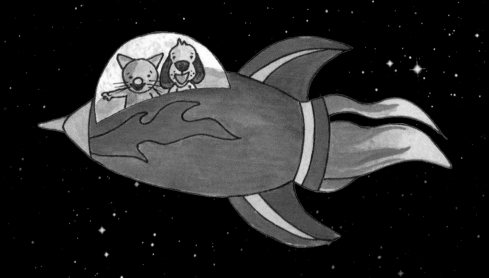

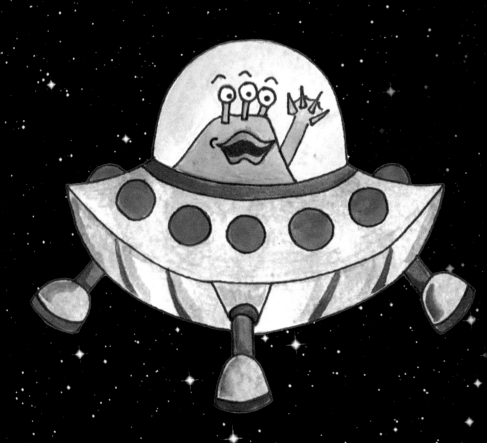

# We see a U.F.O!

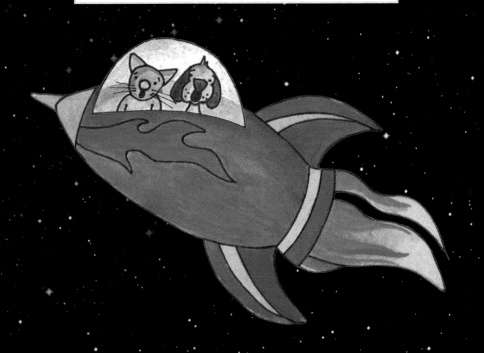

11

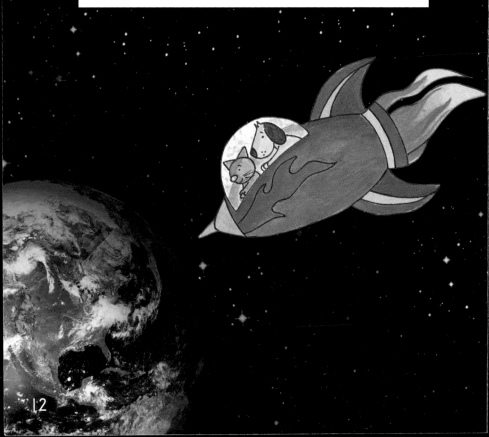

We are going home!